ALLYN & BACON

VideoWorkshop

A COURSE TAILORED VIDEO LEARNING SYSTEM

Introduction to Communication
Student Learning Guide with CD-ROM
Version 2.0

prepared by

Kathryn Dindia
University of Wisconsin

PEARSON

Boston   New York San Francisco
Mexico City Montreal Toronto London Madrid Munich Paris
Hong Kong Singapore Tokyo Cape Town Sydney

ISBN   0-205-43901-2

Printed in the United States of America

10 9 8 7 6   09 08 07

Student Learning Guide
Table of Contents

INTRODUCTION

Welcome to the *Allyn & Bacon VideoWorkshop for Introduction to Communication, Version 2.0*! This video based learning system is specifically designed to improve your education and make it fun!

VideoWorkshop includes a CD-ROM with course specific video clips and your *Student Learning Guide*. *VideoWorkshop* contains 18 units that are designed to be a useful extension and application of information of content that you are studying in your Introduction to Communication class. An assortment of questions in the *Student Learning Guide* is designed to stimulate further application and analysis of communication concepts and techniques.

Your CD-ROM that accompanies the *Student Learning Guide* features course-specific video footage on varied topics. The *Student Learning Guide* includes a video summary of clips on your CD-ROM.

Your *Student Learning Guide* also includes unit learning objectives, review paragraphs, video summaries, observation questions, "Next Step" questions, multiple choice questions, and weblinks. All questions have been designed to encourage in-depth thought and encourage class discussion.

You will also find a correlation grid in your *Student Learning Guide* that connects chapters from Allyn & Bacon's Introduction to Communication textbooks to the 18 learning units on your CD-ROM and in your *Student Learning Guide*.

The *VideoWorkshop* may be used as a source for individualized learning, or for collaborative learning. Either way, this interactive experience is certain to heighten your awareness, understanding, and integration of communication content in an exciting, nontraditional way. Have fun!

CORRELATION GRID CONNECTING
CHAPTERS TO MODULES

#	Concept	Beebe, et al. Communication 2e	DeVito, Essentials 5e	DeVito, Human Comm 9e	Seiler & Beall Communication 6e
1	Self-concept	Chapter 2	Chapter 2	Chapter 6	Chapter 3
2	Self-esteem	Chapter 2	Chapter 2	Chapter 6	Chapter 3
3	Self-disclosure	Chapter 7	Chapter 2	Chapter 6	Chapter 13
4	Perception Checking	Chapter 2	Chapter 3	Chapter 4	Chapter 2
5	Denotation-Connotation	Chapter 3	Chapter 3	Chapter 5	Chapter 4
6	Abstraction	Chapter 3	Chapter 3	Chapter 5	Chapter 4
7	Nonverbal	Chapter 4	Chapter 4	Chapter 6	Chapter 5
8	Listening	Chapter 5	Chapter	Chapter 4	Chapter 6
9	Interpersonal Conflict	Chapter 8	Chapter 8	Chapter 7	Chapter 14
10	Group Decision Making	Chapters 9 & 10	Chapter 10	Chapters 9 & 10	Chapters 15 & 16
11	Types of Groups	Chapters 9 & 10	Chapter9	Chapters 9 & 10	Chapters 15 & 16
12	Cultural contexts	Chapter 6	Chapter 6		
13	Organization	Chapter 12	Chapter 12	Chapter 16	Chapter 11
14	Style	Chapter 13	Chapter 13	Chapter 17	Chapter 12
15	Informative	Chapter 14	Chapter 14	Chapter 18	Chapter 13
16	Visual Aids	Chapter 13 & 14	Chapter 14	Chapter 16	Chapter 10
17	Persuasive	Chapter 15	Chapter 15	Chapter 19	Chapter 14
18	Evidence	Chapter 15	Chapter 11	Chapter 19	Chapter 14

Unit One
Communication and the Self
Communication and Self-Concept

Objectives
Some factors in self-concept development focus on activities associated with the evaluations and responses of others. Some factors focus on the person and her/his self-awareness and evaluations.

- Recognize and identify the behaviors through which Kathy displays her self-concept and factors of its development.
- Note the ways in which others challenge and influence self-concept.
- Identify relationships between self-concept and the attitudes, beliefs, and values Kathy communicates.

Review
Self-concept is an ever-changing process of how you perceive yourself: your feelings and thoughts about your strengths and weaknesses, and your abilities and limitations. It is based on your self-awareness of your identity and is expressed via your subjective descriptions of who you think you are and how you see yourself as a person.

Self-concept develops from communication with others—our associations with groups, the roles we assume, the image others have of you (looking glass self), comparisons between yourself and others (social comparison), your cultural experiences (particularly gender roles and the influences of ethnicity and socio-economic factors), your own self evaluations and labels, and the various ways that others respond to you and your behavior.

Your self concept is reflected in the attitudes, beliefs, and values you hold.

Video
Kathy appears very clear about the relationships between her self-concept and the name she will use after marriage. Her friends differ over the issue. What effects do their opinions have on Kathy's self-concept? Why?

Observations

- Kathy notes a number of factors that contribute to her sense of self. What are they? Are they primarily based on self-evaluations or evaluations by others?

  _____

  _____

  _____

- After Kathy notes the above, she shows a different set of factors. What are they? Do they support or undermine her previously articulated sense of self?

  _____

  _____

  _____

- Which attitudes, beliefs, and values appear to be most evident in Kathy's talk?

  _____

  _____

  _____

Next Step

- Write a response for Kathy that is a direct defense of her self-concept, rather than a more general statement of her views on the situation.

  _____

  _____

  _____

- Could Kathy's friends question the wisdom of her planned name change without seeming to attack her self-concept? What might they say?

_____

_____

_____

Quiz

1. Which factor of self-concept is most crucial?
    a. cultural teachings
    b. significant others' images of you
    c. your self-interpretations and evaluations
    d. your social comparisons with others
    e. All of the above

2. Factors that influence self-concept in childhood have the same influence later in life.
    a. true
    b. false

3. Select the correct saying
    a. Our attitudes shape our behavior, but not our core self-concept.
    b. Looking to others to help us define our self-concept is generally a mistake.
    c. Communicating cross-culturally can change assumptions about self-concepts.

Web

Communication in new media environments promises to present interesting challenges to what we know about identity development. Communication professor Mark Giese published an article that examines how people represent themselves in online interactions in "electronic communities."

"Self without Body: Textual Self-Representation in an Electronic Community," published in *First Monday*, a peer-reviewed Internet journal:

http://www.firstmonday.dk/issues/issue3_4/giese/

Unit Two
Communication and the Self
Communicating Self-Esteem

Objectives

Self-esteem is one of the primary components of self-concept. Self-esteem deals with emotions (how we feel about ourselves), so interactions with other people involving our self-esteem can be "charged" events.

- Notice the way that Kathy's expressions of feelings for herself influence the ways she responds to gender expectations.
- Notice the way that Kathy's expressions of feelings for herself influence the ways she responds to conflict.
- Note that when her friend challenges Kathy's decision about changing her name, the conflict that emerges could damage Kathy's self-esteem. Does it?

Review

Self-esteem refers to the way you feel about yourself—how much you like yourself, how valuable a person you think you are, and how competent you think you are. Your feelings and attitudes about yourself reflect the value you place on yourself. Your self-esteem can reflect your daily view of yourself.

Video

Kathy's self-esteem appears to be strong and positive. The conversation raises issues about her decision and challenges some of her attitudes, beliefs, and values about identity work.

Observations

- At a number of points, one of Kathy's male friends "makes fun" of her married name (Fudd). How does she respond to his inferences? Does her response support her self-esteem? How so?

_____

_____

_____

- Kathy's friend is very emphatic over the seriousness of the challenge to Kathy's identity posed by the proposed name change. How does Kathy's response treat the perceived threat?

_____

_____

_____

Next Step

- Either in a small group discussion, or in a thought paper, discuss the implications to self-esteem brought about by traditions surrounding names after marriage. List the "standard" American options and consider the implications to both parties in the union.

_____

_____

_____

- Investigate and describe the post-marriage naming traditions that are different than the "standard" American mode in which the woman keeps her "given" name and changes her "family" name.

_____

_____

_____

Quiz

1. Self-esteem is
    a. our mental picture of ourselves or our social identity.
    b. made up of beliefs that prevent you from building meaningful relationships.
    c. the human ability to think about what we're doing while we're doing it.
    d. the picture you have of yourself in a particular situation.
    e. None of the above

2. In American culture, high self-esteem is associated with the fulfillment of qualities ascribed to gender (e.g., independence for men, connectedness for women).
    a. true
    b. false

3. Nurturing people
    a. are to be avoided, as they can damage your self-esteem.
    b. are especially helpful at times when your self-esteem is damaged.
    c. will engage in "pity parties" that will help you alter negative behaviors.
    d. All of the above

Web

On the Valdosa State University Web site, Dr. William Huitt and others feature a number of topics related to their interests in educational psychology:

http://chiron.valdosta.edu/whuitt/edpsyindx.html

On the following page, self-esteem and self-concept are defined and discussed. Additional references are provided:

http://chiron.valdosta.edu/whuitt/col/regsys/self.html

Unit Three
Communication and the Self
Self-Disclosure in Interpersonal Communication

Objectives

Self-disclosure is a complex process that is strongly related to the development of interpersonal relationships. Communicators manage a number of features when involved in self-disclosure. To better understand self-disclosure and its effects, you should be able to:

- define self-disclosure
- know the results of empirical research on
    o self-disclosure and relationship development
    o reciprocity of self-disclosure
    o sex differences in self-disclosure
    o self-disclosure and liking
- appreciate the value to interpersonal relationship development of the gradual and reciprocal nature of self-disclosure.

Review

Self-disclosure is defined as verbally revealing information about yourself to others, including thoughts, feelings, and experiences. Self-disclosure varies in breadth and depth. Depth of self-disclosure ranges from relatively non-intimate biographic-demographic information (name, where you live, where you went to school, etc.), to disclosure of your attitudes, beliefs, values, and behaviors, to the sharing of your innermost feelings about yourself. Sometimes discussing matters about people who are close to you constitutes self-disclosure; however, common gossip about others is not considered self-disclosure.

Self-disclosure is related to relationship development. According to the Social Penetration Model, self-disclosure gradually increases in breadth and depth as a relationship develops. According to this model, self-disclosure is based on an analysis of costs and rewards; we self-disclose when we believe the benefits will outweigh the costs, and we refrain from self-disclosure when we believe the costs will outweigh the rewards.

Self-disclosure is related to liking. We like people who self-disclose to us, except when they engage in inappropriate (too intimate or too negative) self-disclosure. We disclose to people we like. We like others as a result of disclosing to them except when the other person does not respond with acceptance and support.

Self-disclosure is reciprocal. Sidney Jourard said, "disclosure begets disclosure" and referred to this as the "dyadic effect." Research on reciprocity of self-disclosure indicates that self-disclosure is generally reciprocal, except for inappropriate self-disclosure that is unlikely to be reciprocated.

Student Learning Guide

Video
Jamie's friend, Emma, has some serious news to share about her mother's health. Although it takes some time for the two to work up to the really important information, we learn a lot about their relationship as they interact.

Observations

- Note the way that small talk is a prelude to big talk. Jamie and Emma share information about dorm food and a mutual friend in ways that are not really self-disclosive, or if they are, they are low-level self-disclosures.

- When Emma discloses her mother's medical condition, notice how talk about another person can be self-disclosive. Emma doesn't share self-disclosures about her feelings until later in the conversation. Note to yourself when she shifts to personal information about self.

- Chart the points at which the conversation features reciprocal and gradual escalation of self-disclosures.

_____

_____

_____

_____

_____

Next Step

- Jamie asked Emma for details about Emma's mother's illness and listened intently. This focus was important; however, Jamie did not inquire about Emma's feelings over the situation. Likewise, though Emma detailed her mother's situation in a disclosive way, she barely talked about her feelings.

8

- Rewrite their dialogue after Emma discloses her mother's medical condition. Craft appropriate and effective ways for Jamie to seek information about Emma's feelings.

_____

_____

_____

_____

_____

Quiz

1. Select the correct statement. In general:
   a. we like people who self-disclose to us.
   b. we disclose to people we like.
   c. we like others as a result of disclosing to them.
   d. All of the above

2. In general, self-disclosure is reciprocal
   a. true
   b. false

3. Explain how self-disclosure during relationship development may be described, by using the analogy of an onion and its skin.

_____

_____

_____

_____

Web

Allyn & Bacon's *Communication Studies* Web site offers useful information and activities. Find there a unit on self-disclosure that includes definitions, concept discussions, a quick quiz, and an interactive activity:

http://www.abacon.com/commstudies/interpersonal/indisclosure.html

Unit Four
Perception
Effective Perception Checking

Objectives

Perception is a universal, yet individual, process. Each person experiences and interprets the world differently from others. Clarifying your perceptions, aligning these with others, and noting perceptual differences are important for effective communication.

- learn to validate perception-based assumptions by asking questions about your observations and interpretations and those of others.
- note the difference between describing external events and internal interpretations.
- practice formulating "perception checks" that offer others opportunities to help you clarify meanings.

Review

Perception is a process through which humans attend to, select, organize, interpret, and remember stimulating phenomena. Although all people are constantly involved in perception and aspects of the process are sometimes similar across individuals (especially among closely related members of families or cultural groups), each person perceives the world in unique ways that are open to a number of influences. It is difficult for us to know what and how each other perceives. Making our perceptions clear to others is an important part of effective communication and mutual understanding.

Through perception checking, we give others access to descriptions of what we think we've experienced (we describe the stimuli) and to our interpretations (we describe our feelings). Then we offer them an opportunity to correct us, to add their interpretations, or to validate our perceptions.

Video

Jamie and Dave do not agree as to how much work and time they should put into their joint project. As they talk, they clarify perceptions of the importance of and their motivations for the activity.

Observations

- Dave asks Jamie about her grades and scores. He then reveals his. Note how Jamie struggles seeing the relevance of Dave's attempt at displaying his perception of the situation.

- Jamie gets Dave to check her perception about Dr. Smith's grading procedures. Notice how she includes a description of what she has observed, as well as describing how she feels about the stimuli.

- Note Dave's response to Jamie's perception. Is it validation or contradiction? Why?

_____

_____

_____

Next step

- Complete the following rewrite of a portion of their conversation in a way that produces clear and efficient perception checks.

Jamie:

(Describes the behavioral stimuli): Dave, it looks to me that you are:

_____

_____

_____

(Describes her feelings): When you do this, I:

_____

_____

_____

Jamie, continued:
     (Checks the perception):

_____

_____

_____

Dave:
     (Describes the behavioral stimuli): Well Jamie, it sounds to me like you are:

_____

_____

_____

(Describes his feelings): When you say this, I:

_____

_____

_____

(Checks the perception):

_____

_____

_____

Quiz

1. You should always check your perceptions directly with the person to whom you are speaking. Avoid indirect perception checking.
    a. true
    b. false

2. The purpose(s) for perception checking is to
    a. check the accuracy of your perceptions and attributions.
    b. reduce uncertainty by further exploring others' thoughts and feelings.
    c. help you sharpen your initial perception toward accuracy.
    d. all of the above

3. Select the correct statement
    a. Perception is a function of the situation and the people's behavior we are perceiving.
    b. Evaluations should be made as soon as possible after initial impressions; first impressions are best.
    c. Personal biases seldom interfere with perception.
    d. None of the above

Web

The Institute for Management Excellence offers practical tools for business and corporate clients and publishes an online newsletter. The August 1997 issue provides practical information for improving verbal skills, particularly "Listening Skills–A key element to learning to communicate well" which provides exercises and examples of perception checking:

http://www.itstime.com/aug97a.htm

Unit Five
Verbal Communication
Meaning: Denotation and Connotation

Objectives

Verbal communication presents a paradox as meanings are determined by the complex intermixing of widely shared conventions with personal and idiosyncratic practices. This unit will help you clarify important distinctions between taken-for-granted linguistic assumptions and meanings-in-use, by asking you to:

- note the differences in a communication scene between the denotative and connotative meanings of words.
- recognize implications to relationships and interactions that can be caused by differences in meanings.
- notice how people attempt to use connotative meanings as though they are denotative.

Review

Words have connotative and denotative meanings. Denotation is the generally accepted dictionary definition through which words are taken to be literal and about content. People who use a word usually know its denotative meaning.

When we use words, we are also using their connotative meanings, perhaps even more so than denotation. Connotation refers to the personal and subjective meanings each person has for words and sayings. Connotative meaning communicates much of language's emotional content.

Video

Sarah's eagerly awaited date, Patrick, has either said that "he is really interested" in Sarah or that he "finds her interesting." These words, "interested" and "interesting," are, well, interesting.

Observations

Sarah's roommate revealed that date did not like Sarah's class presentation. Sarah notes that her roommate told her that Patrick is "really interested" in her. Sarah discovers that, in spite of other factors, her date finds her "interesting."

- Sarah uses the term, "really interested in me," while Sarah's roommate uses the term, "finds you interesting," as though they both know what each means—denotatively. What is meant by each terms' denotative meaning?

  _____

  _____

  _____

- What connotative meaning does Sarah attach to the term her roommate uses in this context?

  _____

  _____

  _____

- What connotative meaning does Sarah's roommate attach to the term she uses?

  _____

  _____

  _____

Next Step

Write dialogue for Sarah's roommate that follows Sarah saying "Patrick is really interested in me." Use the talk to clarify the situation by investigating what Sarah meant in her thinking. As part of the talk, clarify the mistaken assumption about Patrick's feelings toward the class presentation and his subsequent continued interest in dating Sarah.

_____

_____

_____

_____

_____

Quiz

1. A group of people get together and publish a manual of terms related to the highly technical work that they do. The purpose of the manual is to define the terms they often use on the job, especially for clients and other outsiders with and for whom they work. This effort is an attempt to
   a. further develop the connotative nature of their specialized language usages.
   b. build on language's facility for denotation.
   c. make it more difficult for "outsiders" to understand the ways the group speaks.
   d. improve the abstract nature of denotation to increase the ability of denotative terms to work as technical language in their work.

2. When interactants carry on everyday conversations, they proceed as though all parties understand their talk. This assumption
    a. underscores the fact that denotation is the primary mode of meaning for everyday conversation.
    b. shows that misunderstanding does not often occur in everyday communication because it deals with very straightforward meanings.
    c. illustrates the paradox that we often use connotative meanings as though they are denotative in nature.
    d. All of the above

3. As the number of people who agree over the connotative meaning of a word increases, the meaning of the word shifts toward denotation.
    a. true
    b. false

Web

Mick Underwood sponsors the *Communication, Cultural and Media Studies* (*CCMS*) Web site, a valuable resource featuring a wide range of information communication-related issues. In particular, there is an excellent section on meaning, including much about the nature of denotation:

http://www.cultsock.ndirect.co.uk/MUHome/cshtml/semiomean/meaning1.html

Unit Six
Verbal Communication
Meaning: Concrete and Abstract Language

Objectives

Language can be about specific objects and actions in the world or be about concepts and interpretations. Learning language flexibility is a key verbal competency.

- note the differences between concrete and abstract language.
- be able to move sayings up and down the ladder of abstraction.
- appreciate the benefits of concrete and abstract language.

Review

General Semanticists Alfred Korzybski and S. I. Hiyakawa fostered interest in the varying degrees of concreteness (abstraction) available for word use. Concrete words are used when speaking about specific things that can be pointed to or physically experienced. Communication using concrete words leaves little room for disagreement, and when there are differences of opinion, they can usually be solved by pointing to the specific object and its features. Abstract words are symbols for ideas, qualities, interpretations, and relationships. Their meanings depend on the experiences and intentions of the person using them. Effective communicators use both concrete and abstract language, but they do so in appropriately by matching the level of abstraction to needs of particular communication events.

Video

Sarah's roommate tells her that Patrick hated Sarah's presentation. But was it the presentation that he disliked? Or Sarah? Or, something else?

Observations

- Sarah's roommate says "Patrick didn't really like your Heidegger presentation…in fact, he hated it." Is this saying concrete or abstract?

_____

_____

_____

- Sarah's roommate says that Patrick said, "I hate Heidegger; he's a Nazi." Is this saying concrete or abstract?

_____

_____

_____

- Which of the two sayings was more helpful in explaining Patrick's relative interest in Sarah? Explain your answer.

_____

_____

_____

Next Step

- Take the following saying from this unit and make it concrete: Patrick didn't like Sarah's presentation.

_____

_____

_____

Quiz

1. The distinction between concrete and abstract words is the same as the distinction between denotation and connotation.
   a. true
   b. false

2. When deciding between concrete and abstract words, communicators should
   a. always use concrete language; otherwise, listeners are apt to misunderstand.
   b. always use abstract language; otherwise, speakers will be plain and boring.
   c. mix in some abstract language as a way to "spice up" talk that is otherwise concrete.
   d. choose words based on situational requirements (for example, when precision is required, use concrete language; when connection with feelings is required, use abstract words).

3. Discuss the ways that referring to specific objects is an illustration of how the verbal concept "climbing down the abstraction ladder" works.

   _____

   _____

   _____

Web

The Institute of General Semantics pursues the continued study of the ideas popularized by Alfred Korzybski and S.I. Hiyakawa. The site includes a section titled, "General Semantics Basic Formulations:"

http://www.general-semantics.org/

Unit Seven
Nonverbal Communication
The Functions of Nonverbal Communication

Objectives

Nonverbal communication plays an important role in human communication. Researchers have estimated that anywhere from 65% to 90% of communication is nonverbal.

As a result of this unit, students should be able to:
- identify the channels of nonverbal communication and their related functions
- appreciate the importance of nonverbal communication in everyday communication.

Review

Communication is both verbal and nonverbal. Nonverbal communication refers to everything we use to communicate with other than words. Nonverbal communication works in combination with verbal communication. Nonverbal cues substitute for, complement, contradict, repeat and regulate verbal communication. This type of communication is more ambiguous than verbal communication. Verbal communication is discrete; words have a beginning and an end. Nonverbal communication is continuous; we don't stop communicating nonverbally when we stop talking. Unlike verbal communication, which involves one channel, nonverbal communication is multi-channeled. Some of the channels of nonverbal communication are body movements and gestures, physical appearance, facial expressions, eye movements, touch, space, and vocal cues (not what you say but how you say it). Nonverbal cues serve a variety of functions. For example, kinesics (body movement and gestures) have been divided into five categories and corresponding functions.
  o Emblems: gestures that directly translate words or phrases (e.g., the peace sign).
  o Illustrators: gestures that accompany and "illustrate" verbal messages (e.g., a circular hand movement to describe a circle).
  o Affect displays: gestures that communicate emotional meaning (e.g., expressions of happiness).
  o Regulators: facial expressions and hand gestures that monitor, maintain, or control the speaking of another (e.g., raising your hand when you want to speak
  o Adaptors: gestures that satisfy some need (e.g., tapping your foot).
Your textbook identifies a number of other nonverbal cues and their related functions.

Video

The video shows a group of men and women. See if you can figure out what these men and women are doing based on their nonverbal cues.

Student Learning Guide

Observations

- Watch the video with the sound turned off and discuss your impressions about what is happening in the video based on the nonverbal cues. Then play the video, with the volume on, and compare your impressions of what is happening in the video when you have access to both the verbal and nonverbal cues to when you only had access to the nonverbal cues. Indicate the in what ways this video clip demonstrates nonverbal communication as ambiguous.

_____

_____

_____

- Now watch the video clip again and concentrate on body movement and gestures. Stop the video whenever you identify a body movement or gesture. In the table below, identify the body movement and label its type and function (emblem, illustrators, affect display, regulators, and adaptors).

Nonverbal Cue	Category (emblem, illustrator, affect display, regulator, adaptor)	Time on Tape

- In addition to body movements and gestures, there are a number of other nonverbal cues on the video clip that include facial expressions, touch, space, physical appearance, and vocalic cues. Write down some of the nonverbal cues you see in the video, the function of the nonverbal cue, and the time the behavior occurs. Do this for at least 5 types of the nonverbal cues discussed in your textbook. Use the following table to record the nonverbal cues and how they function or what they communicate.

Nonverbal Cue	Function	Time on Tape

Quiz

1.   Nonverbal communication is
    a.   Ambiguous.
    b.   Continuous.
    c.   multi-channeled.
    d.   All of the above

2.   Nonverbal communication _____ verbal communication.
    a.   substitutes for
    b.   Repeats
    c.   contradicts
    d.   regulates
    e.   All of the above

3.   Shaking your head up and down to communicate "yes" is an example of an:
    a.   emblem.
    b.   illustrator.
    c.   affect display.
    d.   regulator.
    e.   adaptor.

Web
Link to hundreds of topics on nonverbal communication at:

http://www3.usal.es/~nonverbal/miscell/miscell2.htm

Unit Eight
Interpersonal Communication
Supportive Listening

Objectives

Supportive listening is a complex skill that is strongly related to interpersonal communication effectiveness and the quality of interpersonal relationships. To better understand listening and its effects, students should be able to:

- differentiate between understanding, sympathy and empathy.
- define and provide examples of :
  - o back-channel cues.
  - o Questions.
  - o paraphrasing.
- appreciate the value of supportive listening to interpersonal communication and interpersonal relationships.

Review

We listen for different purposes. Sometime we listen for enjoyment. Sometimes we listen for information. Other times we listen to communicate empathy and support. Supportive listening requires effectively employ complex listening skills. First, the listener needs to provide verbal and nonverbal cues that communicate, "I'm listening," including eye contact, appropriate facial expressions, backchannel cues ("yeah," "right," "oh," and "uh-huh"), and appropriate verbal responses (comments and questions that demonstrate that you are paying attention and listening). Second, the listener needs to ask questions (to clarify the message, to probe for additional information, to check the listener's understanding of the speaker's message, and to elicit the speaker's feelings). Third, the listener needs to communicate understanding, sympathy, and support, and, if possible, empathy. Empathy is to feel what another person is feeling. It is different from understanding (that is to cognitively understand what another person is feeling). It is different from sympathy (that is to feel pity or compassion for another person's trouble or suffering). To communicate understanding, the listener needs to accurately paraphrase the speaker's message (restate in your own words what the speaker said). To communicate support, the listener needs to acknowledge that the speaker is feeling bad and to offer help and comfort. To communicate empathy, the listener needs to verbally and nonverbally communicate that he/she is feeling what the speaker is feeling. It is not always possible to feel empathy but we can nevertheless communicate understanding, sympathy, and support.

Video

Jamie's friend, Emma, has some serious news to share about her mother's health. It takes some time for the two of them to work up to the really important information, and we learn a lot about their relationship as they interact.

Observations

- What does Jamie communicate, verbally and nonverbally, that elicits Emma's self-disclosure?

_____

_____

_____

- When Emma says, "I wish I could be there with her and my dad", why does Jamie respond with, "It is probably easier this way"?

_____

_____

_____

- Why does Jamie respond to Emma's description of her mother's medical condition with a story about her aunt's medical condition?

_____

_____

_____

- What other things does Jamie do verbally and nonverbally to communicate empathy and support?

_____

_____

_____

Next Step

- What else could Jamie do to communicate empathy?

_____

_____

_____

- Rewrite the dialogue from when Jamie says, "I sure do miss my mom's cooking." Craft appropriate and effective ways for Jamie to communicate empathy and support that include ways to elicit Emma's feelings.

_____

_____

_____

_____

_____

Quiz

1. Active listening is the process of responding verbally and nonverbally to a speaker's message.
   a. true
   b. false

2. To feel empathy is to feel sorry for someone.
   a. true
   b. false

3. To summarize the speaker's message in your own words is referred to as
   a. back channel cues or minimal responses.
   b. active listening.
   c. paraphrase.
   d. perception check.

Web
This is the website of the International Listening Association. It includes Listening Exercises, Listening Tests & Assessments, Listening Factoids, a Convention Paper Resource Center and more.

http://www.listen.org/

Dr. Larry Alan Nadig, Ph.D., a clinical psychologist and marriage and family therapist, provides a number of useful Guidelines on Effective Communication, Healthy Relationships & Successful Living including *Tips on Effective Listening:*

http://www.drnadig.com/listening.htm

Take this *Listening Self-Assessment:*

http://www.highgain.com/SELF/index.php3

Complete this survey of the *Top 10 Listening Habits* by Dr. Rick Bommelje:

http://www.listencoach.com/

There are several good articles on listening at *The CEO Refresher* including *Deep Listening: How can it make a difference for you?, Engaged Listening and Inquiry, and Listen Up ... and Speak Out! How You Can Use Conversations to Improve Organizational Effectiveness:*
http://www.refresher.com/!deeplistening.html
http://www.refresher.com/!jswengaged.html
http://www.refresher.com/!conversations.html

Unit Nine
Interpersonal Communication
Managing Interpersonal Conflict

Objectives

Your ability to engage in the most effective communication behaviors during conflict can play an important role in keeping conflicts constructive. Through this unit, students will learn to:

- define conflict.
- identify five styles of responding to conflict.
- become aware of your own conflict style.
- be able to use the conflict style that is most appropriate in a particular conflict.

Review

According to William Wilmot and Joyce Hocker, authors of *Interpersonal Conflict*, conflict is an expressed struggle between two or more interdependent parties who perceive incompatible goals, scarce resources, and interference from others in achieving goals.

Conflict styles are habitual responses or behaviors that people use in conflict. We tend to rely on the same tactics when responding to conflict. Some of us are avoiders, others are confronters, and so on. But, by always responding to conflict in the same way, we may not be responding to conflict in the most effective manner. According to Wilmot and Hocker, constructive conflict management depends on our ability to choose from a variety of conflict styles and tactics in order to respond to a particular conflict with the most effective conflict behaviors. Thus, it is important to learn the different conflict styles and use them consciously and intentionally, rather than habitually responding to conflict in the same way.

Conflict styles vary on two dimensions: assertiveness (or concern for self), and cooperativeness (or concern for other). Several authors have identified five conflict styles located in this two-dimensional space:

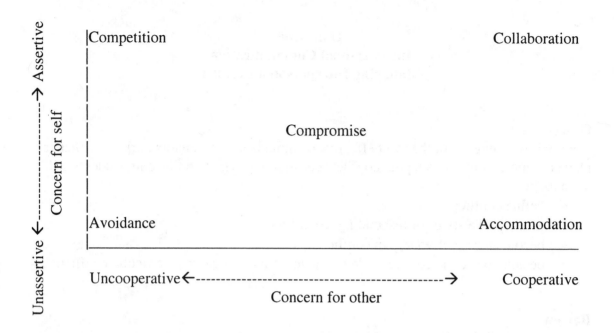

Avoidance is unassertive and uncooperative. It is characterized by withdrawing from the partner (physical avoidance) or avoiding the conflict (psychological avoidance). Conflict can be avoided by denying there is conflict, by being evasive, by avoiding the topic and changing the topic, by being noncommittal, and by irreverent remarks (making light of the conflict).

Accommodation is unassertive and cooperative. It is characterized by giving up or giving in, by denying your needs, and by expressing your desire for peace and harmony.

Competition is assertive and uncooperative. It is characterized by a number of behaviors including personal criticism, rejection of or disagreement with the other person's statements, hostile requests, demands, arguments, threats, hostile jokes, teasing or sarcasm, blaming the partner, and denying responsibility. In its extreme form, competition involves verbal and/or physical abuse.

Compromise is moderately assertive and cooperative. It involves finding a middle ground, a solution that will partially satisfy everyone involved. Compromise is characterized by appealing to fairness and suggesting trade-offs.

Collaboration is assertive and cooperative. It is characterized by descriptive (versus evaluative) statements, self-disclosure, qualifying statements, eliciting self-disclosure, eliciting criticism, supportive statements (communicating understanding, support, acceptance, positive regard for the partner, shared interests and goals), concessions, and accepting responsibility.

There is a web link to an online survey at the end of this unit. It allows you to measure your conflict style.

Video

Two individuals are trying to finish a paper by its deadline. The conflict arises when one student prefers to do a mediocre job and shoot for a "C" and the other student wants an "A." The male student tries to convince his female partner that doing "decently" is acceptable; while the female student feels her performance is important to her self-concept.

Observations

- Watch the video clip and pay attention to the conflict issue and the conflict-handling behaviors employed in the clip.

- Identify the elements of conflict in the video clip. What is the expressed struggle? Who are the interdependent parties? What are the perceived incompatible goals? What are the scare resources? And what is the source of interference in achieving these goals?

_____

_____

_____

_____

_____

- What conflict management styles are used by Dave and Jaime to try and reach a solution?

_____

_____

_____

_____

- Do you think the conflict is resolved in a constructive manner?

_____

_____

_____

_____

Next Step

- Continue the dialog for this conversation by taking up where it left off. In this continuing dialog demonstrate the use of collaboration and/or compromise to resolve the conflict.

_____

_____

_____

_____

_____

- Think about some of the bigger conflicts in your relationships. What types of conflicts were they? How did you try to resolve them?

_____

_____

_____

- Based on your answer to the above question, do you see any of the conflict styles present in how you respond to conflict?

_____

_____

_____

Quiz

1.   What must be present for there to an interpersonal conflict?

_____

_____

_____

2.   Collaboration is the most constructive communication style and we should always respond to conflict with collaboration
      a. true
      b. false

3.   Physically or psychologically withdrawing from conflicts, a strategy that can produce mixed results for conflict management is called _____.

Web

For a more detailed description of the five conflict styles and to take an online conflict styles inventory that will indicate your conflict style go to:

http://www.viha.ca/hr/conflict_mgmt/conflict_styles.htm

Unit Ten
Small Group Communication
Critical Thinking and Group Decisions

Objectives

Many people report difficulties communicating and working effectively in small groups. Small groups, when used properly, can be very efficient problem solvers and decision makers. Many times group members often do not use proper problem-solving procedures. Through this unit, students will learn to:

- recognize ineffective small group problem-solving behaviors.
- adapt dysfunctional behaviors to take advantage of the standard agenda for problem solving.
- increase your confidence in effective group work by isolating advantages from decision-making guided by problem solving.

Review

The "standard agenda" or "problem-solving sequence" was adapted from John Dewey's suggestions as to how reflective thinking works. Later, group theorists adapted the method. The steps (in various orders, depending on the theorist) include:
- Identify the problem by asking questions of fact, value, and/or policy.
- Analyze the problem by researching its history, causes, effects, symptoms, etc.
- Establish criteria for evaluating potential solutions.
- Generate creative solutions.
- Test solutions with the criteria and select the best solution.
- Implement trial runs of the selected solution(s); evaluate and fine-tune solutions.

Video

Shanenna and Dishari have more than one problem. Not only do they have to prepare a class presentation, but also they have to deal with Victoria's schedule, attitude, and plans.

Observations

- Note that even though the three agree (rather tentatively) to do a better presentation, they have not used an efficient procedure for that decision. More than likely, their problem is not solved. This is apparent from Victoria's uninterested response.

- Notice that Victoria actually comes closer to following the standard agenda for problem solving than do her companions.

Next Step

- Write dialogue for Shanenna and Dishari that follows the standard agenda for problem solving as a way to convince Victoria that more time and effort should be put into their presentation.

_____

_____

_____

_____

_____

_____

_____

Quiz

1.   All group problem solving must use the standard agenda in order to be rational.
      a. true
      b. false

2.   Theorists order "generating potential solutions" and "establishing criteria for evaluating solutions" in a variety of ways. Why?
      a. Generating criteria before potential solutions can limit creativity and constrain the range of potential solutions.
      b. Generating solutions before establishing criteria can result in many "potential" solutions that are just not practical.
      c. Generating criteria before potential solutions can help groups evaluate potential solutions against real criteria, rather than merely using criteria that prop up decisions that have already been made.
      d. All of the above

3.   Write the following statement as an open question:
      "Small groups are better off using an organized set of problem-solving procedures than not using organized steps."

      _____

      _____

Web

Carter McNamara, MBA, Ph. D., of Authenticity Consulting, LLC, developed most of the materials found at Web site for The Management Assistance Program for Nonprofits (MAP) in St. Paul, Minnesota. The site, Free Management Library (SM), includes excellent resources about the basic nature of groups and how these develop, including numerous subtopics about various types of groups (teams, focus groups, decision-making groups, etc.):

http://www.mapnp.org/library/

http://www.mapnp.org/library/grp_skll/grp_skll.htm

Unit Eleven
Small Group Communication
Communication and Types of Groups

Objectives
There is no single best way to hold meetings and accomplish group work. Establishing the best procedures depends on the type of group, the nature of the task, and other factors.

- increase your sensitivity to the variety of factors that determine group type and task dimensions.
- fine-tune your ability to adjust group meeting procedures flexibility, depending on circumstances.
- note the damage done when group procedures get at cross-purposes with member needs and preferences.

Review
Group communication occurs for a variety of reasons in a number of settings. The type of group designates, to some degree, the procedures that should occur. Some groups focus on generating ideas (brainstorming), and others focus on personal growth (therapy or catharsis). Groups can share information (learning/study or focus groups) or focus on solving problems and making decisions through work (committees and teams) or politics (parties or movements). Of course, sometimes people function in groups for social and relational reasons (primary groups such as families or social groups), rather than trying to achieve specific goals.

Video
Victoria is late, but she is still not ready to start the meeting. Dishari and Shanenna have good reason to want to get right down to business. Can this group either be fun or do good work?

Student Learning Guide

Observations

- Despite her late arrival, Victoria would like a period of socializing at the start of the meeting. Note how the others cut her off, curtail the social opportunity, and, in the process, set up an adversarial situation.

- From the other perspective, note that Victoria is not sensitive to the implications of being late.

- Victoria suggests the sort of decision making and presentation that Dishari and Shanenna have already ruled out. However, when the three discuss their visions for the presentation, Victoria details reasons for her view, while the other two simply disagree with her and dictate the outcome based on majority rule.

Next Step

- Write dialogue for Dishari and Shanenna that would welcome Victoria. Make clear their negative assessment of her late arrival, yet make room for some socializing at the meeting.

- Write dialogue for Dishari and Shanenna that lays out a constructive process for decision making. They have two decisions to make: First, they have to decide what sort of presentation to make and, second, they have to decide on the procedures they will use for laying out the presentation.

Quiz

1. Primary groups are the decision-making bodies that mean the most to our daily work lives.
    a. true
    b. false

2. Focus groups make persuasive announcements and serve as implementation committees for larger groups that have made decisions.
    a. true
    b. false

3. Virtual groups, online chat groups, and mailing list groups can benefit from using many of the same procedures, as do face-to-face groups.
    a. true
    b. false

Web

Carter McNamara, MBA, Ph. D., of Authenticity Consulting, LLC, developed most of the materials found at Web site for The Management Assistance Program for Nonprofits (MAP) in St. Paul, Minnesota. The site, *Free Management Library* (SM), includes excellent resources about the basic nature of groups and how these develop, including numerous subtopics about various types of groups (teams, focus groups, decision-making groups, etc.):

http://www.mapnp.org/library/

http://www.mapnp.org/library/grp_skll/grp_skll.htm

Unit Twelve
Cultural Contexts
Culture in Contexts of Communication

Objectives

Recognizing important cultural differences in contexts is only the first step to effective communication. Interactants must adapt their behaviors appropriately, while maintaining outcome goals. Three dimensions are particularly important.

- identify where interactants might be placed on a scale between high and low context orientation.
- identify where interactants might be placed on a masculine vs. feminine scale.
- identify where interactants might be placed on a individualistic to collectivistic culture scale.
- suggest behavior adaptations to key differences among interactants.

Review

Culture may be defined as the knowledge, experience, attitudes, beliefs, values, meanings, hierarchies, practices, roles, artifacts, and notions about the universe (space and time) shared by a group of people and handed down from one generation to another.

America is becoming increasingly diverse; communication situations often include a cultural dimension. The greater our differences, the more difficult it is to interpret verbal and nonverbal symbols and to listen accurately to the messages of others and to adapt our messages for others.

Video

Shanenna and Dishari have differing communication styles and do not share some perspectives about the course. However, they are going to work together; we'll see how well.

Observations

- Identify where these interactants might be placed on a scale between high and low context orientation.

Shanenna's Cultural Context Orientation

low _____ high

Dishari's Cultural Context Orientation

low _____ high

- Identify where these interactants might be placed on a masculine vs. feminine scale.

Shanenna's Masculine vs. Feminine Orientation

masculine _____ feminine

Dishari's Masculine vs. Feminine Orientation

masculine _____ feminine

- Identify where these interactants might be placed on a individualistic to collectivistic culture scale.

Shanenna's Individualistic to Collectivistic Culture Orientation

individualistic _____ collectivistic

Dishari's Individualistic to Collectivistic Culture Orientation

individualistic _____ collectivistic

Student Learning Guide

Next Step

- Suggest behavior adaptations to key differences among interactants. For example, how could Shanenna display sensitivity to Dishari's demonstrated need for agreement? How might Dishari adapt to Shenenna's preference for directness?

_____

_____

_____

_____

Quiz

1. Interactants high in ethnocentricism
   a. strive to understand differences rather than to judge these.
   b. assume that on fundamentals like values and beliefs, all reasonable people are very similar.
   c. seek information from others that might lower uncertainty.
   d. All of the above

2. You are at a model United Nations group meeting in which the "representatives" are (actual) ethnic nationals from the represented countries. What kind of culture would the national members be from who think the furniture arrangement in the room doesn't much matter and that the group should get right to work rather than enjoying a social hour prior to the meeting are more likely from a:
   a. High context culture
   b. Low context culture

3. Culture is not a part of a communication transactions in which the interactants are from the same ethnic, socio-economic, gender, and racial grouping.
   a. true
   b. false

Web

The University of Iowa Department of Communication sponsors an extensive repository of Web links to information on a variety of topics. Links to information about cultural studies are provided along with links to information about gender and race issues as these relate to communication:

http://www.uiowa.edu/~commstud/resources/culturalStudies.html

http://www.uiowa.edu/~commstud/resources/GenderMedia/index.html

42

Unit Thirteen
Speaking in Public
Organizing Speech Materials

Objectives
Good speeches have clearly identifiable parts: a beginning, middle, and end. Main points, in the body of the speech, are organized according to predictable patterns. This unit will help you to:

- recognize the value of clearly differentiated parts of public speeches.
- develop flexibility when selecting and applying organizational patterns for main points.
- select organizational patterns for main points in accordance with the logics suggested by speech topics and in line with audience expectations.

Review
There are many organizational issues for speeches. This unit covers two: (1) organizing the parts of the speech and (2) organizational patterns for the main points. A third concern, organizing materials within sections (particularly support materials), is covered in "Persuading with Evidence."

A speech should have a clear beginning, middle, and end. The introduction, body, and conclusion of the speech normally represent those parts. Within the body of the speech, main points (each divided by related subpoints) organize the content of the presentation.

Main points should be organized in a way that makes sense in light of your treatment of the topic and the expectations of the audience. Patterns include cause and effect, problem solution, time sequence, spatial organization, the motivated sequence, structure-function, comparison-contrast, pro-con, advantages-disadvantages, 5W pattern (who, what, where, when, why), and topical organization.

Video
Michael Whitley's speech about *Laserpaint* is an informative speech given in the championship round of an American Forensics Association national tournament. The introduction, body, and conclusion of the speech are clearly marked. Forensic competitors often combine common patterns to organize main points: you'll note, especially, structure-function and comparison-contrast.

Observations

- Write down what Michael says as transitions between the three major sections of the speech (end of the introduction to start of the body and end of the body to the start of the conclusion).

_____

_____

_____

_____

- List the main points in Michael's speech.

_____

_____

_____

_____

- Identify the ways this main point organization demonstrates structure-function. Identify the ways this main point organization functions as comparison-contrast.

_____

_____

_____

_____

Next Step

- Assume the same content/material is used in the speech you prepare. Reorganize your speech using an alternative organizational pattern for main points. Do not use either structure-function or comparison-contrast. For example, how would you organize this speech following a motivated sequence? The more ways you can reorder the speech, the more you will learn about flexibility with main points. One cannot use every pattern on all topics, but many topics can be organized effectively in a number of ways.

_____

_____

_____

_____

_____

Quiz

1. The introduction is the first part of your speech; therefore, you should work on it first. Once you plan how to get off to a good start, the rest of your speech will fall into place.
   a. true
   b. false

2. Organizing your speech provides the following:
   a. The claims in your speech will need support. Organization provides evidence.
   b. Organizational patterns usually make your speech sound structured, constrained, and limited in flexibility.
   c. Speeches with obvious connections and relationships among parts are easier for audiences to follow than are speeches with random order.
   d. All of the above

3. The Motivated Sequence organizational pattern
   a. uses the past, present, and future as central theme.
   b. divides the speech into two major sections (in addition to introduction and conclusion).
   c. breaks speeches into self-evident subdivisions.
   d. includes a visualization step.

Web

Presentations.com features numerous materials for speakers, including a series of articles focused on various approaches to organizing speech materials:

http://www.presentations.com/presentations/creation/organize_archive.jsp

Unit Fourteen
Speaking in Public
Language Choices for Speeches

Objectives

What could be more important to public speaking than the very words that you say?

- learn to select words that facilitate understanding.
- learn to select words that increase message impact.
- learn to avoid word choices and constructions that risk ruining speech impact.

Review

In public speaking, style refers to word choice and arrangement. Speeches combine prepared words with live performance. Selecting and preparing words and phrases carefully and thoroughly can increase communication effectiveness, but what is actually said is sometimes adapted to the needs of the moment. Direct, simple, and clear constructions can help audiences understand the message; vivid, memorable, and pleasing constructions can help "breathe life" into the presentation.

Video

Holly Sisk's topic, "The Need for Correct Hand Washing," persuades about a serious issue within listeners' everyday experience. Her language style upholds the importance of the topic without making it seem overly formal.

Observations

- Note the numerous stylistically interesting choices Holly includes throughout her speech.

- For example, early in the introduction, Holly uses "severe gastro-intestinal discomfort," "a new ingredient," and "a new meaning to ordering the number two." Throughout, her speech, these instances make a telling point and invoke pointed responses from the audience.

- Notice that while this speech could be very technical (after all, it is about bacteria, science, and statistics), Holly's language choices ("eewwweeee," "gross," and "wash up,") keep the speech on a level appropriate to the audience.

Next Step
- Write five sentences describing the poisoning incident in Minnesota that Holly details at the start of the speech. Use one of the five elements of figurative language in each sentence. Write as though you are going to deliver each sentence in a speech on this topic.

Hyperbole:

_____

_____

Metaphor:

_____

_____

Personification:

_____

_____

Simile:

_____

_____

Rhetorical Question:

_____

_____

Quiz

1. Decisions about style should favor "fancy-sounding" words and relatively complex constructions so the audience gets the impression that you really know what you are talking about.
   a. true
   b. false

2. Decisions about style should favor "everyday-sounding" words and constructions so the audience hears you speak as you do in normal conversations.
   a. true
   b. false

3. Changes in American society, especially increases in the use of slang, vulgar and offensive expressions on television and in films, have made the use of these informal ways of speaking acceptable in public speaking situations.
   a. true
   b. false

Web

The "Forest of Rhetoric," *silva rhetoricae,* is an online guide by Dr. Gideon Burton of Brigham Young University dedicated to the hundreds of terms naming figures of speech. The site also provides instruction about many aspects of style:

http://humanities.byu.edu/rhetoric/silva.htm

Student Learning Guide

Unit Fifteen
Informative Speaking
Better Understanding Via Informative Speech

Objectives

Informative speeches function by adjusting new information in ways that effectively increase listener knowledge.

- Note the importance of specific purpose statements in informative speeches. Although informative speeches may contain information that is "news" to listeners, information should not be packaged as a "surprise." The audience should be able to predict what information the speaker will cover and how she/he will go about it.
- Appreciate that although information can lead to new ways of thinking, informative speeches are not designed for persuasive outcomes.
- Critique flaws in main point patterning when these threaten understanding.

Review

Informative speeches increase listener knowledge. These can be about objects, processes, events, people, and ideas/concepts. Informatives can be speeches of description, definition, or demonstration.

Good informative speeches bring information to audiences that they might not already know. These speeches should do so without overwhelming the audience by focusing on the information and by relating new information to old. Informative speakers adjust the level of the information so the audience can follow, understand, remember it, and for the audience to underscore the usefulness of the information.

Video

Michael Lynch carries two main points in his speech. He previews these as part of a very explicit specific purpose statement. Note the informative nature of this presentation.

Observations

- Note that Michael's main point preview is flawed. Although he says that he will talk about (a) two new teaching methods, (b) government programs for progressive learning, and (c) changes in the future of education, his third point is actually covered in his conclusion rather than in a main point.

- Michael primarily uses description and explanation to inform his audience. Note how he supports his description of collaborative learning with a story reported in *Time* magazine.

50

Next Step

- Rewrite the statement of specific purpose and the main point preview in a way that better specifies and clarifies the structure of this speech.

_____

_____

_____

- Indicate places in his speech that Michael could (or should) have used additional evidence in support of his descriptions.

_____

_____

_____

- Assess the effectiveness of this speaker's attempts to bolster his credibility on this topic. Note his early references to his personal experience.

_____

_____

_____

Student Learning Guide

Quiz

1. Speech techniques are not of much use to informative speakers. If the information is really important and "true," it will impact the audience merely because it is so.
   a. true
   b. false

2. The purpose of informative speaking is to increase audience understanding. To that end,
   a. speakers should present a lot of very complex information, because listeners will find this informative.
   b. speakers should present as many facts as they can fit into the available timeframe.
   c. citing sources for information is not as important in informative speaking as it is in persuasive speaking.
   d. the level of abstraction at which one speaks must be adjusted to that at which the audience can best comprehend the material.

3. You've done some basic research on your topic, but the speech is due tomorrow and you need to rehearse it, so you are writing, rather than doing more research. You don't fully understand the entire subject, but you have some specific information about the part on which you are speaking. You didn't note the sources, so you don't plan citing the evidence directly. You aren't sure that the point you are making is true, but the speech you've written sounds good enough as you rehearse it. This situation raises major questions about:

   _____

   _____

   _____

Web

You are most likely learning about informative speaking in a speech communication or communication class. Other academic disciplines also have interests in informative speaking. For example, the fact that one often writes the speech before delivering it finds teachers of English or writing interested in informative speaking.

The Writing Center at Colorado State University provides extensive coverage of the process of preparing informative speeches:

http://writing.colostate.edu/references/speaking/infomod/

Unit Sixteen
Informative Speaking:
How to use PowerPoint (Electronic) Visual Aids

Objectives

Electronic visual aides are no different from other visual aids. The speaker is simply replacing another form of a visual aid with an electronic visual aid. The same rules apply to electronic visual aids that apply to other forms of visual aids. Visual aids are used to help the audience visualize what the speaker is saying. In this unit:

- students will learn to ensure that the speaker's message, not the electronic visual aid, is most important.

Review

Informative speakers often use audio/visual aids to help the audience visualize, understand, and remember important aspects of the speech. PowerPoint slides, or other electronic visual aids, should follow the rules of all audio/visual aids. A few of these rules are:

1. Just as the speaker's delivery should focus attention on the speech, not the speaker, the electronic visual aid should focus audience attention on the speech, not on the PowerPoint slides. Avoid slides that include lots of words, numbers, and figures, lots of irrelevant sounds or movement. These all encourage the audience to read the slide rather than listen to the speaker.
2. Text on visual aids, including PowerPoint slides, should be simple, readable, and uncluttered.
    - A. Rules for keeping text on PowerPoint slides simple:
        - i. The fewer the words, the better. No more than 3 lines of text and six words per line on the slide (or 6 lines of text and 3 words per line – not including title).
        - ii. Use key words or phrases – not sentences.
        - iii. Capitalize only the first word of each line.
    - B. Rules for keeping text readable:
        - i. Type size should be $\geq$ 28 points.
        - ii. Avoid hard-to-read fonts.
        - iii. Use numbers when points are numbered
    - C. Rules for keeping text visually uncluttered:
        - i. include only the key numbers on graphs/charts.
        - ii. Use a header to avoid repeating the same word.
        - iii. Leave a good amount of white space on the slide.
3. The speaker should refer to the PowerPoint slides to describe, explain and elaborate about what is on the PowerPoint slide.
4. The speaker should never read from PowerPoint slides. PowerPoint slides are audience visual aids-- not speaker notes. Maintain eye contact with the audience.

Student Learning Guide

Video

Kristina Shaw's informative speech is on "Van Gogh's Incredible Life," a perfect speech for electronic visual aids. These electronic visual aids help the audience visualize the painter and his paintings. As you watch the presentation, pay attention to the PowerPoint slides. Think about what PowerPoint slides you would use if you were giving this speech.

Observations

- What visual aids does Kristina use and what points is she trying to visualize or help the audience understand with these visual aids?

_____

_____

_____

_____

- Kristina primarily uses electronic visual aids to point out the chronological time periods of Van Gogh's life. How could these slides be more effective?

_____

_____

_____

_____

- Kristina uses electronic visual aids to display two pictures of Van Gogh (for the audience to see what he looks like), and four of his paintings. While these pictures are effective, what else would you like to have seen visually displayed during this speech?

_____

_____

_____

_____

Next Step
- Redesign the slides that contain the time periods of Van Gogh's life so that they include a short phrase illustrating the main feature of each phase of his life.

- Indicate places in the speech where Kristina should have used additional visual aids in support of her description of Van Gogh's life.

_____

_____

_____

_____

- Assess the effectiveness of this speaker's visual aids in terms of the six rules for electronic presentations listed at the beginning of this unit.

_____

_____

_____

_____

Quiz
1. PowerPoint slides are different from other visual aids and, thus, different rules should be applied for designing PowerPoint slides.
   a. true
   b. false

2. The text and graphics on PowerPoint slides should be
   a. simple.
   b. readable.
   c. uncluttered.
   d. All of the above

3. It is acceptable for the speaker to read from the PowerPoint slides when delivering a PowerPoint presentation.
   a. true
   b. false

Web

The Virtual Presentation Assistant, maintained by the Communication Studies Department at the University of Kansas, provides helpful tips and techniques for using visual aids while public speaking. This site provides links to other pages that will help you design effective visual aids.

http://www.ukans.edu/cwis/units/coms2/vpa/vpa7.htm

Unit Seventeen
Persuasive Speaking
Setting Goals for Persuasive Speeches

Objectives
Persuasive speaking requires an artful mix of materials and approaches. Effective persuasive speakers surround their audiences with solid motivations for change. Increase your ability to use each of the three kinds of persuasive material by:

- bolstering your credibility in topic-relevant ways.
- showing effective methods for giving good reasons, particularly via the presentation of evidence and source citation.
- appealing with emotion in order to engage the audience's feelings without alienating listeners.

Review
Persuasive speaking attempts to reinforce or change listeners by getting them to adopt, discontinue, avoid, or continue an attitude, belief, value, or behavior. Effective persuasive speakers establish their credibility on issues, convince the audience their claims are reasonable, and appeal to the emotions of the audience as ways to induce change. Persuasive speeches deal with questions of fact, definition, policy, and value. Listener involvement in the topic is important, as is the degree to which the speech goal is in line with audience members' current thinking and their perceived need to change.

Video
Heath Rainbolt's speech about body image distortion is particularly persuasive by his high personal involvement. Note his strong use of organization, the presentation of lots of credible evidence, and the speech's telling emotional appeals. Heath doesn't depend on his credibility alone.

Observations
- Note the way that Heath uses problem-solution organization for his main points.

- Make note of the numerous times, and ways, that Heath includes the audience by using the terms, "us," "we," and "you." This is a speech about the audience, though they would not normally think so.

- Perhaps the most effective persuasive element comes when Heath presents evidence that implies people who are free from eating disorders fall into body image distortion. This method applies the topic to all audience members. Detail the way he makes this connection.

_____

_____

_____

_____

Next Step

- Write a brief outline for this speech and change the organization pattern to the motivated sequence while removing the personal involvement element (the speaker no longer has an eating disorder). Note the changes that would be required if this were to remain an effective speech.

_____

_____

_____

_____

Quiz

1. If a speaker is persuasive enough, s/he can convince audiences to change their fundamental values as a result of a given speech.
    a. true
    b. false

2. Heath's specific purposes are to examine body image distortion by looking at its definition, it's impact on society, and ways to beat it. The goal of his speech focuses on
    a. question of fact.
    b. question of value.
    c. question of policy.

3. Which kinds of motivations does Heath use?
    a. Dissonance
    b. Needs
    c. Fear
    d. All of the above

Web

Allyn & Bacon's *Communication Studies* Web site features an interactive activity titled "Persuasive Speaking on Legislative Topics." The purpose of this activity is to use government documents on the World Wide Web to gather information about a topic that is under consideration by lawmakers:

http://www.abacon.com/pubspeak/exercise/congtop.html

Unit Eighteen
Persuasive Speaking
Persuading With Evidence

Objectives
Informative and persuasive speeches benefit from the presentation of evidence that supports claims that audience members may find questionable.

- identify the claim-evidence structure in speeches to "catch" unsupported claims or insufficient support.
- recognize a variety of evidence types and consider factors indicating the quality and usability of support factors.
- learn to cite sources accurately, efficiently, and effectively.

Review
Speeches benefit from the presentation of material that audiences find acceptable as support for messages. Speakers do well to identify each claim of fact, definition, value, or policy that they make and use audience analysis to decide if the claim is already acceptable (or taken-for-granted). Speakers should provide support for any claims that are not agreed to.

Audiences must understand the material and find the information credible; they must understand how the information connects to the speaker's claims (find it relevant), and they must think that the speaker presents enough good reasons for them to accept a given claim.

Whenever support that is not common knowledge is offered, accurate source citations should be used both to bolster the effect of the evidence and to enable the audience to judge the quality of the material. Types of support include illustrations, descriptions and explanations, definitions, analogies, statistics, expert testimony, and physical evidence.

Video
Ben Lohman's speech about identity theft (name fraud) can only be successful if he convinces the audience that the problem is significant in both scope and impact. Note how he uses evidence to persuade listeners to be concerned based on evidence indicating that they are not immune from the problem. Also, each support is properly cited.

Observations

- List the four instances of supporting materials that Ben uses in the introduction of his speech. What type of evidence is each?

_____

_____

_____

_____

- Note the oral citations Ben uses for his evidence. What elements are stressed?

_____

_____

_____

_____

- What are the most prominent types of support used in this speech?

_____

_____

_____

_____

Next Step

- Outline the material covered in the first main point of this speech, especially noting the relationships between claims and the data that supports these.

_____

_____

_____

_____

Quiz

1. Oral citations for materials drawn from Web sites should include the URL (Web address) where the material was found.
    a. true
    b. false

2. Celebrities make good sources for expert testimony
    a. because they are well-known, regardless of the subject on which they are quoted.
    b. when they are quoted regarding subjects within their expertise (actors on acting, doctors on medicine, basketball players on basketball, etc.).
    c. only when they are not speaking about the kind of work they do; too much bias results when celebrities speak about their own expertise.
    d. none of the above.

3. It is not necessary to cite sources for information and support when

    _____

    _____

Web

The Cornell School of Law sponsors *The Legal Information Institute* (*LII*), a site often identified as the most linked to Web resource in the field of law. Although using evidence in public speaking does not have to follow laws that apply in court settings, learning about how evidence is handled in the American system of justice helps speakers fine-tune their abilities to manage support materials. LII provides a number of links to resources about the use of evidence:

http://www.law.cornell.edu/topics/evidence.html

NOTES

NOTES

NOTES

NOTES

NOTES

NOTES

NOTES

NOTES

NOTES

NOTES